Chloe Cloud
AND THE
Friendly Fog!

WRITTEN BY ELAYNE HEANEY   ILLUSTRATED BY PAULA REEL

To David,
for making my heart happy
each and every single day.
Thank you for making me a mummy.

Created and Written by Elayne Heaney
laineyheaney@gmail.com

Illustrations and Design by Paula Reel
paulreel@gmail.com

Printed by GPS Colour, Belfast
www.GPScolour.co.uk

First Printing, 2020

ISBN 978-1-5272-7696-3

Published by Wonderfully Weathery Books
Dublin

wonderfullyweatherybooks@gmail.com
www.wonderfullyweatherybook.com

Chloe Cloud come out to play,
What are you going to bring us today?
Will you bring rain or will it be snow?
Will you help paint the sky
with a pretty rainbow?

Meet **CHLOE CLOUD,**

She is a cloud called Chloe.

She lives in a place called **WEATHERVILLE**
and looks white and snowy.

Chloe and her family float beneath the sunshine,

sailing around the **WORLD**

having the very best time.

Welcome to
Weatherville

Chloe is happy, caring and FUN, always giggling away under the HOT, SHINING SUN.

She floats all day long and sings as she flies,

WHOOSHING HERE,
WHOOSHING THERE
across the blue skies.

You see, the thing about clouds is they love to whoosh about, gazing down at the world, watching people run about.

Clouds love to play tricks on the people below, to keep them guessing about the weather – will it rain, **WILL IT SNOW?**

Sometimes on a sunny day,

Chloe has the **BIGGEST HOOT,** floating right over the sun to make the humans **TOOT!**

Bobby Breeze is Chloe's friend

and helps her with this fun,

by pushing her about the sky until the day is done.

Bobby is a

BREEZY GUY

and gentle as a mouse,

but if he's really in a mood his gusts can

SHAKE A HOUSE!

One day while they were PLAYING,
Chloe let out a big cry, "Look, Bobby, quick – something's
FALLEN FROM THE SKY!"

BOBBY stopped to take a look
to see if Chloe was right,
and sure enough made a YELP
when he saw the terrible sight.

"I DO BELIEVE IT IS A CLOUD!"

said Chloe with a scream,

"IT'S FALLEN TO THE EARTH BELOW AND HAS LANDED IN THAT STREAM!

We need to go get them help and check they're alright, they must be so very scared and shaking with the fright!"

"I'm off to call **AIR RESCUE**

to see can they come

and help us rescue that poor cloud who's fallen

on its **BUM!**"

All the clouds started gathering

to hear the awful news,

watching Air Rescue get to work –

THEY HAD
NO TIME TO LOSE!

CHLOE CLOUD and **BOBBY BREEZE**
made their way down too,
and then they saw the fallen cloud
surrounded by the crew.

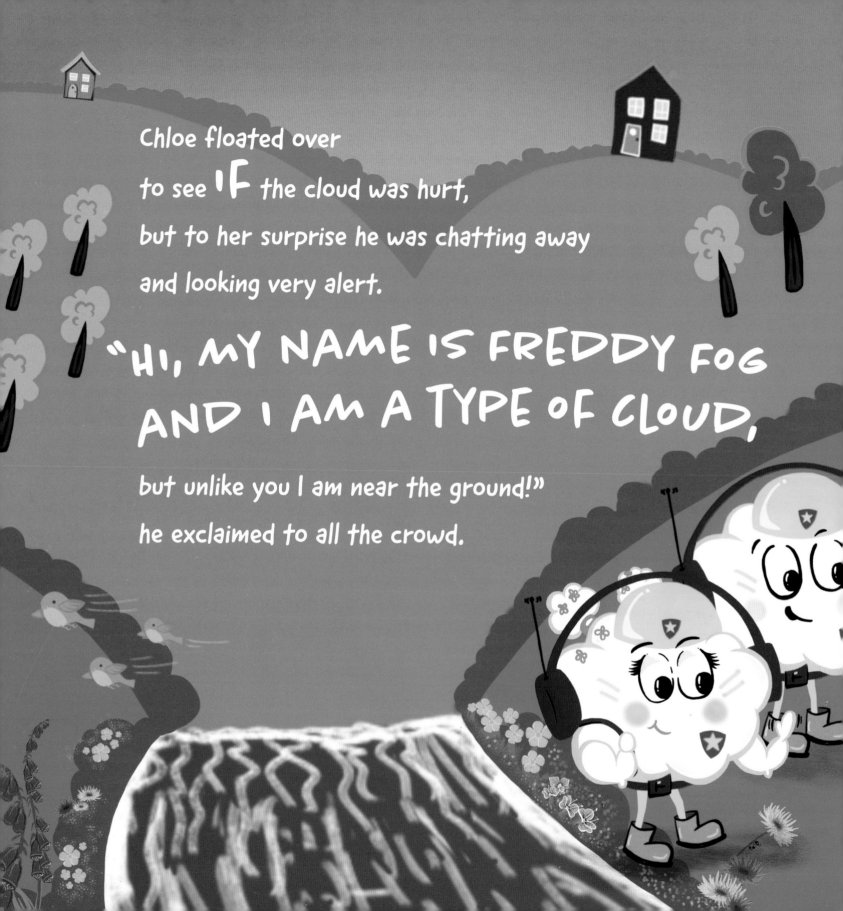

Chloe floated over
to see **IF** the cloud was hurt,
but to her surprise he was chatting away
and looking very alert.

"HI, MY NAME IS FREDDY FOG
AND I AM A TYPE OF CLOUD,

but unlike you I am near the ground!"
he exclaimed to all the crowd.

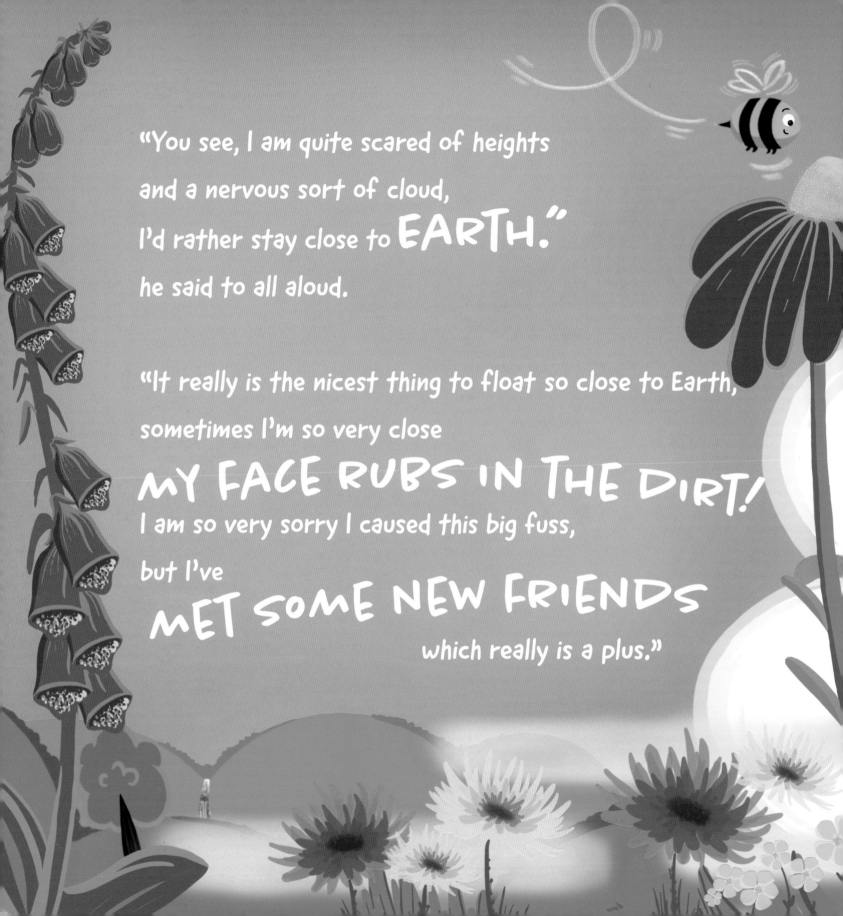

"You see, I am quite scared of heights
and a nervous sort of cloud,
I'd rather stay close to EARTH."
he said to all aloud.

"It really is the nicest thing to float so close to Earth,
sometimes I'm so very close

MY FACE RUBS IN THE DIRT!

I am so very sorry I caused this big fuss,

but I've

MET SOME NEW FRIENDS

which really is a plus."

"I know that I might look like you
but I don't think the same,
but we can still be friends if you want
to stay and
PLAY A GAME?".

Chloe Cloud and Bobby Breeze
started **GIGGLING** out loud
to think they'd caused such **CHAOS**
about this
NOT SO FALLEN CLOUD.

FREDDY FOG was overjoyed at finding these new friends – who'd have thought that such a misunderstanding would have this happy end.

So remember, if you see a **HAZY CLOUD** lying on the ground near you, you'll know it's just a nervous fog trying to

SMELL THE MORNING DEW!

FACTS ABOUT CLOUDS!

WHAT ARE CLOUDS MADE OF?

Clouds are made out of water – little tiny drops of water! A single cloud can contain millions of water-drops! Clouds form when the sun pulls water up from the ground into the sky. This is called evaporation. When the water gets there, the cooler air in the sky pulls the water together and TA-DA! You have clouds. This is called condensation.

TYPES OF CLOUDS

STRATUS clouds are flat and look like sheets of paper floating in the sky. See if you can spot them on your next walk. They are normally a grey colour and cover most of the sky.

CIRRUS clouds are thin, stringy clouds – they are always the highest clouds in the sky – if you spot them when you're out and about ask your grown-up to take a photo and tag me @wonderfullyweathery books.

CUMULUS clouds are big, white, puffy and fluffy looking clouds – they are everyone's favourite cloud. Chloe Cloud is a cumulus cloud as she has a flat base and rounded top.